You Are Your
STRONG

To my children, Nicole and Ben, who are my Strong—DD

To my children, who made me strong; to my husband and parents, for sharing your Strong with others; and to my sister, one of the strongest people I know—JZ

Magination Press

American Psychological Association
750 First Street NE
Washington, DC 20002

Magination Press is a registered trademark of the American Psychological Association. Order books here: www.apa.org/pubs/magination, or call 1-800-374-2721.

Book design by Gwen Grafft
Printed by Worzalla, Stevens Point, WI

Library of Congress Cataloging-in-Publication Data

Names: Dufayet, Danielle, author. | Zivoin, Jennifer, illustrator.
Title: You are your strong / by Danielle Dufayet ; illustrated by Jennifer Zivoin.
Description: Washington, DC : Magination Press, [2019] | "American
    Psychological Association." | Summary: A child explains how to find your
    "Strong," conquering fear, anger, and other emotions or emotional
    reactions either alone or with help. Includes note to parents and caregivers.
Identifiers: LCCN 2018009934| ISBN 9781433829390 (hardcover) | ISBN
    1433829398 (hardcover)
Subjects: | CYAC: Emotions—Fiction. | Self-control—Fiction.
Classification: LCC PZ7.1.D8337 You 2019 | DDC [E]—dc23 LC record available at
https://urldefense.proofpoint.com/v2/url?u=https-3A__lccn.loc.gov_2018009934&d=
DwIFAg&c=XuwJK26h77xqxpbZGgbjkdqHiCAgI8ShbCmQt4lrFlM&r=-
JHK41InHLZmadgoIUDYfA&m=urg53oteY8HbFnwtvpj_J6l-hPFOMKXFKzU1xNIPNLs&s=
Ta6fQSHgs62SBXEF0Hhtb8XbC214gw_GPdsbjgjdVWs&e=

Manufactured in the United States of America
10 9 8 7 6 5 4 3 2 1

You Are Your STRONG

by **Danielle Dufayet**

illustrated by **Jennifer Zivoin**

Magination Press • Washington, DC • American Psychological Association

When puppy's woofs turn into whimpers,
Worry whispers in my ears.

Momma puts her arms around me and tells me everything will be OK. Her **Calm** becomes my inner strength, my Strong. And Worry washes away.

When waves curl and CRASH and
SCARED creeps in,

Papa puts me on his shoulders and shows me Brave.
His **BRAVE** becomes my Strong and Scared slips away.

If I can't find my stuffed Lovey,
Sad sprinkles my heart.

Grandma rubs my back and listens until the sun shines again.
Her *Love* becomes my Strong and Sad fades away.

When someone knocks my blocks and **Mad** stomps in,

I want to scream and hit.

Grandpa helps me find words instead of shouts.
His *Gentle* becomes my Strong and Mad melts away.

You are more than just your feelings.
Inside you, your **Strong** is a light that shines like the sun.

But sometimes you have to find your Strong all by yourself.

Like if I am full of **Worry** when Sissy's late.

I find **Calm** by sitting outside and breathing blue.
Or I whistle a tune until Worry washes away.

If I'm shivering with **SCARED** about monsters and dark,

I find **BRAVE** by making up a funny story.

Or I rat-a-tap-tap my favorite song

until Scared slips away.

If my balloon goes SWOOSH and Sad pours in,
I find Love by helping someone else.
Or I draw with my brightest colors until Sad fades away.

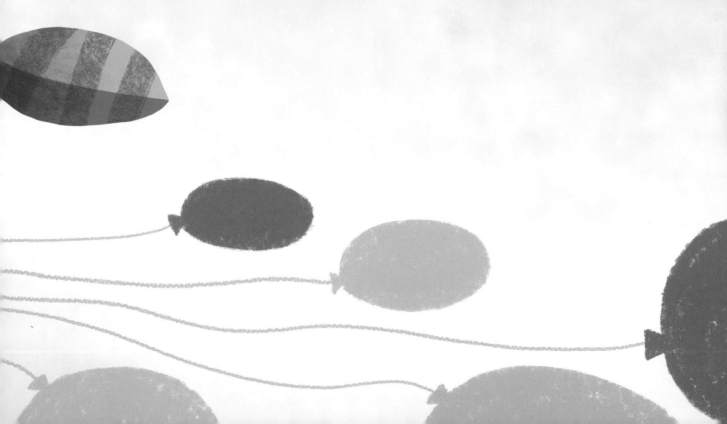

When someone grabs my Bobo and **Mad** charges in,
I sometimes have to yell into a pillow
before I can find words to get the hot out.

Then, I dive into an adventure until Mad melts away, and I find **Gentle** again.

Your **Strong** helps you roar like a lion.
It tells you *you'll get through this*.
It whispers *just keep trying*.
Sometimes your Strong helps others find their Strong.
Sharing Strong makes it grow.

Your **Strong** is like a treasure inside of you.

Sometimes you might need
a little help finding it.

And sometimes you just need
to close your eyes and remember,

it's always there, burning bright.
You are your Strong.

Note to Parents and Caregivers
by Julia Martin Burch, PhD

Strong emotions are an essential part of being human. They enable us to love, feel joy, and connect with others. However, strong emotions—particularly uncomfortable feelings like sadness, anger, and fear—can be painful and hard to cope with. Children are not born knowing how to handle these powerful emotions. Perhaps you can think of examples from just this week when your own child struggled with anger or sadness! However, learning to navigate their own emotions is one of the most important developmental tasks young children face. As a parent or caregiver, there is much you can do to help your child build skills to cope with big emotions and to become their own Strong.

Validate Your Child's Emotions...

One of the most important things a caregiver can do to support an upset child is to validate their feelings. In the context of emotions, validation means communicating to your child that you hear that they are upset and that it is okay to feel that way. It is important to note that validating your child's strong emotions does not imply that you accept or approve of their behaviors following that emotion. For example, if your child is feeling angry about someone knocking their blocks over and yells or knocks over their playmate's blocks in retaliation, you might say "Given how hard you worked on your block tower, I understand that you're feeling angry." By saying this, you are not communicating "...and it's great that you knocked over John's blocks!" but instead are simply sharing that you see that they are upset and that the emotion makes sense to you.

Labeling your child's emotions helps to increase their emotional self-awareness. It also helps them begin to make connections between their experiences (*my tower was knocked over*) and emotions (*and now I feel mad*). This is a critical building block of learning to regulate emotions. Validation can also be very soothing to a child dealing with a painful feeling; however, for this to occur it is important to resist the urge to jump straight from validation to problem solving.

...And Pause Before Problem Solving

It is almost always more effective to wait to talk through a difficult situation with your child when they are calm, rather than in the heat of a strong emotion. To highlight this point, think of a situation in your own life in which you felt strong emotions. How effectively could you take in language and think through your actions while still feeling intense emotions? Probably not very well! Children are the same, only to a greater degree because of their not-yet-fully-developed brains! So validate your child's difficult emotion first and help them calm down (see "Develop a Coping Kit" for ideas for how to do this). Later, when your child is calmer, you can discuss their emotion-related actions, give a consequence if needed, and problem solve for how they can cope more skillfully the next time they are very upset. Of course, if your child's strong emotion has caused them to do something unsafe, it is important to respond immediately—for example, by separating them from the playmate they hit. Once your child is calm, you can return to the situation and talk through how they might handle those feelings the next time they occur.

It is the most natural urge in the world to want to immediately respond to or "fix" your child's strong emotions. For example, if a child is feeling sad about their lost Lovey, as in the story, it is understandable that many parents would feel the urge to quickly offer to get the child a new stuffed animal to soothe their sadness. However, when parents immediately attempt to address the source of their child's strong emotion, the child misses out on a chance to learn that emotions come and go like waves and that they are capable of riding out an emotion and feeling calm on the other side.

Model Coping Skills

Children learn how to handle their emotions by watching how you handle your own. Just as the worried young boy in the story becomes calm upon seeing his mother act calmly, your child learns how to cope with big emotions by following your lead. When you experience an emotion, particularly one that's painful or hard to feel, consider labeling that emotion for your child and describing how you will cope with it. For example, you might say "I'm feeling annoyed right now because of the bad traffic. I am going to take some deep breaths and play some music I like to help myself stay cool and calm." Sharing your emotions in appropriate situations (i.e., when your child can understand the situation and will not feel scared or unsafe themselves knowing that you are upset) can normalize big emotions for children. It also can teach them that there is no shame in feeling sad or worried and that it is possible to calm those emotions down. Additionally, watching you use your own coping skills gives children ideas of strategies they might try themselves when they're upset.

Develop a Coping Kit

It can be scary to feel out of control of one's emotions. By knowing that they can handle whatever emotion they experience, children feel empowered and strong. One great way to teach your child to manage big feelings is to teach them coping skills. The children in this story try many strategies to cope with worry, fear, and sadness, including whistling, making up silly stories, and helping others. Similarly, you can help your own child begin to build up a repertoire of coping skills and activities to try when they feel a big emotion that they want to calm down.

Often, helpful coping skills involve acting opposite to the urges a child feels following a strong emotion. For example, when children feel scared, their fear urges them to retreat and hide. By doing the opposite, whether it's being brave on Dad's shoulders or dancing around the scary attic, children learn that they can make their fear smaller and feel calm. As another example, anger typically urges children to lash out and yell. By finding words or diving into another adventure as in the story, children learn that they do not have to act on their anger. Praise your child whenever they attempt to use a coping skill, whether or not it was ultimately helpful, as this will encourage them to continue to try. Over time, your child will learn that they can cope with big emotions and can find their strong, calm place—no matter what the world may bring.

When to Seek Support

Some children take longer to develop emotion-regulation skills than others, and a learning curve is to be expected in any child developing a new ability. However, if your child's powerful emotions consistently interfere with their functioning (such as hard-to-control anger leading them to lose many friends, or worry keeping them from doing the things they want to do), consider seeking additional help. Consult with a licensed psychologist or other mental health professional who specializes in cognitive behavioral therapy (CBT) for children.

Julia Martin Burch, PhD, is a staff psychologist at the McLean Anxiety Mastery Program at McLean Hospital in Boston. Dr. Martin Burch completed her training at Fairleigh Dickinson University and Massachusetts General Hospital/Harvard Medical School. She works with children, teens, and parents, and specializes in cognitive behavioral therapy for anxiety, obsessive compulsive, and related disorders.

About the Author

Danielle Dufayet teaches English and public speaking/self-empowerment classes for kids. She has a bachelor's in English literature and a master's in psychology. She has always been drawn to the beauty and simplicity of picture books and attracted by their powerful psychological impact on young minds. She believes that books are magic little gems that can change one's life. She lives in San Jose, California. Visit danielledufayetbooks.com.

About the Illustrator

Jennifer Zivoin is trained in media ranging from figure drawing to virtual reality, and earned her bachelor of arts degree with highest distinction from the honors division of Indiana University. Jennifer worked as a graphic designer and creative director before finding her artistic niche in children's books. She has illustrated over 30 books, including *Something Happened in Our Town: A Child's Story About Racial Injustice* and *A World of Pausabilities: An Exercise in Mindfulness*. Jennifer lives in Carmel, Indiana. Visit JZArtworks.com.

About Magination Press

Magination Press is an imprint of the American Psychological Association, the largest scientific and professional organization representing psychologists in the United States and the largest association of psychologists worldwide.